The Special Guest

Steve Smallman

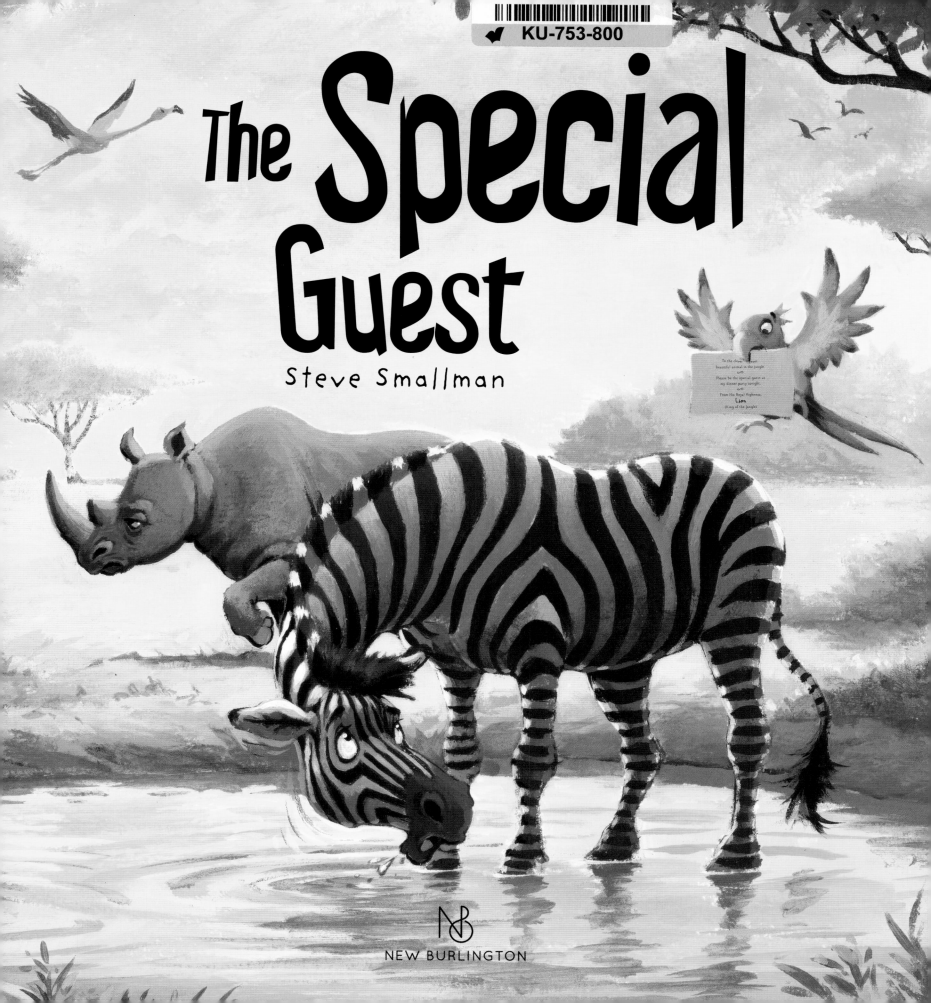

NEW BURLINGTON

"LION?" cried Elephant.
"Zebra, you can't go!"

"I MUST go," said Zebra, "I'm the special guest! You're just jealous because you're not clever or beautiful like me!"

"Well... you can't go looking like that!" said Elephant. "You're covered in mud!"

"OH, NO!" cried Zebra, "I'd better have a bath."

And while he did, the invitation blew away...

...and landed on Porcupine.

"To the cleverest, most beautiful
animal in the jungle..."
read Porcupine.

"That's me!
I'll set off straight away."

Invitation
to meet the
King of the Jungle

To the cleverest, most
beautiful animal in the jungle.

Please be the special guest at
my dinner party tonight.

From His Royal Highness,
Lion
(King of the Jungle)

And as he did, the
invitation blew away again.

"I'm all clean," cried Zebra.
"Time to party!"

"Maybe," said Elephant,
"but your mane
is a mess!"

"I'd better
have a haircut,"
said Zebra.

Just then the invitation landed on Rhino.

"To the cleverest, most beautiful animal in the jungle..." read Rhino.

"That's me! I'll set off straight away."

"Now it's party time!" cried Zebra.
"My mane looks marvellous."

"Maybe," said Elephant.
"But your stripes are a disaster!"

"Oh really, Elephant!" cried Zebra. "I'll touch up my stripes but then I'm going."

And as he did, Elephant took some of the paint and ran off!

Lion was lazing in the sun when he heard someone calling from the bushes.

"Your Majesty, your special guest has arrived."

"My plan worked," said Lion.
"It's Zebra!"

"Dinner time!" he growled,
as he pounced over the bush...

...and landed on Porcupine!
"OUCH!" he cried.

Lion was pulling the last prickles out of his bottom when someone in the bushes called,

"Your Majesty, your special guest has arrived."

"It must be Zebra!" said Lion.

"Dinner time!" he growled as he pounced over the bush...

...and landed on Rhino who tossed him into the swamp! **"OUCH!"** cried Lion once again.

Lion had just dragged himself
out of the swamp when
someone in the bushes called:

"Your Majesty, your
special guest
has arrived."

It must be Zebra this time, thought Lion.
He peeped through the bushes to
check and saw... zebra stripes!

"DINNER TIME!"

he growled as he pounced over
the bush, straight onto...

...the biggest zebra bottom ever!

"Dinner time? Lovely!" said Elephant
and sat down.

"But where's the food?" asked Elephant.

"There isn't a dinner party," wailed Lion.
"I just wanted to eat Zebra!"

And Zebra, who had just arrived,
finally realized how silly he'd been.

"Thank you, Elephant," Zebra cried.
"You saved my life!"

"I'm sorry I was
rude to you.

You are very clever and actually
quite beautiful today...
it must be the stripes!"

Next Steps

Show the children the cover. Can they guess what the story is about? Read the title together. Who do they think the 'Special Guest' might be?

Which of the animals is the children's favourite and why?

Elephant is supposed to be Zebra's friend but early in the story Zebra says some very mean things to her. Ask the children how they think Elephant felt. How would they feel if their friends were mean to them?

Elephant tries very hard to stop Zebra from going to the party. Why? Can the children remember everything Elephant made Zebra do?

Ask the children what they think of Lion. What words could they use to describe him? *Is he clever?* And why did he put 'To the cleverest, most beautiful animal in the jungle' on the invitation, and not just 'To Zebra'?

Do the children feel sorry for Lion? After all, he does get prickled, tossed into a swamp and sat upon by an elephant!

At the end of the story, do the children think that Zebra has learnt his lesson?

Ask the children to draw a picture of an elephant with zebra stripes, tiger stripes or leopard spots!